Murray
the Horse

For Evan
My best pal and inspiration – G. P

For Lois, Jack and George – F. R

First published by
Faber & Faber Ltd in 2015
Bloomsbury House
74–77 Great Russell Street
London WC1B 3DA

Typeset by Faber & Faber Ltd
Printed and bound by CPI Group (UK) Ltd, Croydon, CR0 4YY

Text © Gavin Puckett, 2015
Illustrations © Frank Rodgers, 2015

The right of Gavin Puckett and Frank Rodgers to be identified as author
and illustrator of this work respectively has been asserted in accordance
with Section 77 of the Copyright, Designs and Patents Act 1988

A CIP record for this book is
available from the British Library

ISBN 978-0-571-31522-2

FSC
www.fsc.org
MIX
Paper from
responsible sources
FSC® C101712

2 4 6 8 10 9 7 5 3

Murray
the Horse

Gavin Puckett

Illustrated by Frank Rodgers

FABER & FABER

On a warm summer's day at a race track in Surrey,

something **odd** happened to a racehorse called Murray.

The events that unfolded were certainly strange,

    events that by chance caused his whole life to change.

Murray decided – as a young foal –

    to make championship-racing his ultimate goal.

He dreamed of success, of riches and fame;

    dreamed fans the world over would cheer out his name.

He came from a family of true sporting glory,

where triumph and praise was a regular story.

His parents won trophies and medals galore

and hoped beyond hope that their son would win more.

But despite Murray's plans to reach stardom some day,

there was one major problem that stood in his way.

♘ 4 ♘

A difficult hurdle he couldn't get past . . .

Murray the horse wasn't that fast!

He trained as often as any horse could,

but this dutiful racehorse just wasn't that good.

His trainer once dubbed him, **'A racing disaster!'**

claiming that **'*Jockeys* could even run faster!'**

To make matters worse, Murray lived in a stable

with racehorses FAR more athletic and able.

There was **Big Brandy Wilson** and

his brother **Ned Plumb**,

who were cousins of horseracing legend **Red Rum**.

There was **Bucky the stallion** and

Old Reggie Clover,

each of them champions several times over.

But the fastest of all was a racehorse called **Pete**,

who was known to his fans by the name

'Thunder-Feet'.

Compared to these marvels, Murray was small

and had never been trusted by jockeys at all.

Instead, he was used as a ground steward's horse,

carting equipment around the racecourse.

When he worked, they all laughed if he even dared canter,

and they ridiculed him with their teasing and banter.

They treated poor Murray as if he was dirt,

and nobody cared if his feelings got hurt.

The horse sometimes sobbed when he was alone,

but knew his emotions should never be shown –

he was certain the others would take satisfaction,

at seeing a weakness in such a reaction.

Instead he walked round with a smile on his face,

ignoring their comments, still longing to race.

Murray yearned for that chance to make his folks proud.

'I *will* be a racehorse . . . someday!' he vowed.

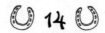 14

One day at the stables, whilst Murray was walking,

he happened to overhear two jockeys talking;

discussing in detail a national race,

planned to be held at *that very place*.

This annual race was prestigious and grand,

and took place on courses all over the land.

 16

Now the *Speed Saddle Cup* was coming to Surrey!

Much to the joy and excitement of Murray.

Soon word had spread and the horses were keen

to get out on the track for their training routines.

Each jockey in camp put their horse through its paces,

hoping they'd win this, the finest of races.

Murray observed from the sidelines in awe,

    at the strength and the grace in the horses he saw.

He daydreamed of how it would be to compete,

    and beat a true favourite like **Thunder-Feet Pete**.

But . . . a spectator was all he seemed destined to be,

    since nobody took Murray seriously.

His cumbersome nature was hard to ignore –

If only he knew what this race had in store!

In no time at all race day was there,

    and the horses had one final chance to prepare.

They took to the fields in an energised flurry;

    cheered by supporters and admired by Murray.

 23

The ground stewards sat in the VIP tent,

    making the most of this special event.

They soaked up the atmosphere feeling excited –

    Murray however, had *not* been invited!

As usual Murray was left all alone

    and expected to watch the big race on his own.

But the horse didn't mind, he had thought up a plan

that would tickle the fancy of any race fan!

Glad to be rid of the stewards and farriers,

Murray mixed with the crowd behind the race barriers.

Now he could savour the breathtaking thrills

and experience the feeling of spine-tingling chills.

Murray picked out a spot in the very front row

and he gazed at the horses, all raring to go!

The racehorses gathered to check out the track,

led by the jockeys perched high on their backs.

Bucky the stallion gave things the once over.

So did **Ned Plumb** and old **Reggie Clover**.

Then . . .

whilst trotting past Murray

quite unfortunately,

Ned tripped in a divet

and twisted his knee!

The onlookers gasped and

could tell by Ned's face –

he was terribly hurt,

he could no longer race.

Ned's jockey, Tom, didn't know what to say.

He just patted Ned's nose as they led him away.

Tom gloomily sighed and he followed behind,

with dreams of *what could have been* filling his mind.

With his head in his hands, Tom wished in his heart

that maybe he'd still get a chance to take part.

He turned one last time to look at the course,

when there in the crowd . . .

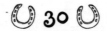 30

Tom spotted a horse!

'That's odd!' exclaimed Tom, thinking out loud.

'Why is a horse all alone in the crowd?'

The *Speed Saddle Cup* was about to take place

and the rest of the horses were all set to race.

Tom raised an eyebrow feeling perplexed,

then grinned as he thought about what to do next.

He quickly adjusted the watch on his wrist;

this was a prospect NOT to be missed!

Perhaps there's still time, thought Tom at a glance

and he hurried on over, seizing his chance.

Murray was shocked when the jockey came near,

tiptoed beside him and spoke in his ear . . .

The horse's nerves tingled and he stared into space,

as Tom asked the question . . .

'Fancy a race?'

The horse blinked his eyes feeling rather dumbfounded,

his knees went all weak and his anxious heart pounded.

Murray tried to stay calm but started to stutter,

bewildered and dazzled by what Tom had uttered.

Then, with a deep breath and a slow, calming sigh,

Murray gained his composure and had one more try.

 35

He looked straight at Tom in his full racing dress

and, fulfilling his dreams, Murray smiled and said . . .

'Yes!'

The jockey was primed and all set to compete;

he checked Murray's legs and examined his feet.

The horse appeared fit; Tom had nothing to lose,

so he called to a stable boy . . .

'Get him some shoes!'

Now most of the time, this type of command

would be something all stable folk would understand.

But of all the workers Tom happened to choose . . .

This new boy had never before fitted shoes!

 38

But before the young lad had a chance to explain,

the jockey was off to announce his campaign.

The stable boy gulped, bemused and befuddled

and he dithered about feeling nervous and puzzled.

The race would soon start and he knew he must hurry,

so he picked up the reins and yelled,

'Quick! Come on, Murray.'

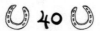 40

The boy led the horse to a small wooden shack

and took down four horseshoes that hung on a rack.

Murray's face beamed as he stood in the hay

and he wondered with joy what his parents would say.

He could see straight away as he lifted his feet;

that these shoes were made for **the racing elite!**

The young lad worked tirelessly, aiming to please,

hammering nails as he held Murray's knees.

The shoes were a good size and fitted quite tight.

But when the boy finished, they didn't feel right.

Nevertheless, Murray limped from the shack,

and met his new jockey next to the track.

As the two made their way to the course to compete,

Murray *knew* things were amiss with his feet.

Each time that his hooves met with the ground,

he felt an incredible urge . . . **to turn round.**

The jockey was curious and started to worry

when he noticed that something was bothering Murray.

'What's up?' questioned Tom with a look of dismay

   as he asked with concern, 'Are you feeling OK?'

Murray just shrugged feeling rather downbeat

   and he glumly replied, 'Something's wrong with my feet!'

Tom checked out his hooves and gave a horrified grunt

   when he realised the horseshoes were on . . .

back-to-front!

But the race would soon start; they had no time to lose . . .

Murray HAD to take part in those back-to-front shoes!

Murray awkwardly trotted to the starting position,

where the spectators scoffed at this new, late addition.

Then a ground steward heckled, whilst giggling

and grinning . . .

**'There's more blooming chance of a
rocking-horse winning!'**

Tom knew too well that they looked out of place,

but he also sensed Murray's desire to race.

As soon as he'd guided his horse to the start,

Tom gently whispered . . . 'Follow your heart!'

Inspired, Murray nodded and took his position,

knowing that *this* was his lifelong ambition.

But rather than facing the course with his head,

he turned **around** and led with his **bottom** instead!

The horses looked stunned and the stewards turned pale . . .

when TOM turned around and held on to his tail.

At first there was silence; not one single word.

Then one of the crowd shouted out: **'That's absurd!'**

A few other comments followed thereafter,

when suddenly . . .

Everyone burst into laughter!

But brave Murray snubbed all the sneering and jeering

and imagined instead the crowd clapping and cheering.

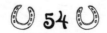

54

He once again smiled, ignoring the flak

and knew in his mind there was no turning back!

When he stood in reverse, (to Murray's delight)

his legs seemed much stronger; his body quite light.

These feelings had never occurred in the past . . .

Incredibly, Murray the racehorse **felt fast!**

Now up stood the race marshal strict as can be

and he lifted his arm for the horses to see.

The competitors tensed in anticipation,

eager to race and perform for the nation.

He blew on his whistle with a clear, sharp blow

and the horses shot off as their jockeys screamed –

Murray charged into action

along the first section,

like a **missile** being fired

in a backwards direction.

His legs were a **blur** and he

galloped with pride,

passing the horses with

each unique stride.

His hooves churned

the grass and they

pounded the ground,

as the crowd

stood in wonder,

not making a sound.

Tom clung to Murray with all of his might,

impressed at the pace of his horse in full flight.

Even Murray himself was amazed by his speed –

and now he was battling hard for the lead!

Soon, there was only *one horse* left to beat.

He could tell from the sound of its hooves it was Pete.

Thunder-Feet Pete turned to see who was second,

(for in his mind victory already beckoned).

But the last thing of all Pete imagined would greet him

was a horse hurtling *backwards* at high speed

to beat him.

So Pete galloped harder, driven by fear,

at the drumming of hooves getting ever so near.

Murray responded and

picked up the pace

and soon his large bottom

drew alongside Pete's face.

Then both jockeys yelled to

encourage their steeds,

when suddenly . . .

Murray the horse took the lead!

The crowd, who went crazy, got up on their feet,

some screaming 'Murray!' and others, 'Go Pete!'

No one before had seen such a race,

with a **back-to-front horse out in first place!**

Pete was now frantic and chomped at his bit;

he was boiling with fury and raging with grit.

'I can't lose!' cried Pete, 'I can't be outclassed!'

But Murray the racehorse was simply **too fast!**

Murray felt glorious, on top of his game

and listened with pride as the crowd cheered **his name.**

He grinned to himself, **overjoyed with his work,**

but when he looked up . . .

He noticed Pete smirk.

How peculiar! *Thought Murray, Thunder-feet's losing.*

What in the world does he find so amusing?

Then down came a heavy, firm slap on his rump;

followed by Tom yelling . . .

'**Yikes!**' Murray shrieked and instinctively lifted

his hind legs as if he was naturally gifted.

His fore legs soon followed with power and flair,

propelling the racehorse high into the air.

The jockey held on and regained his calm poise,

amidst the excitement and spectators' noise.

 73

'How did he do it?' Pete spluttered, not knowing.

'He's backwards and can't even

see where he's going!'

Even Murray was baffled and couldn't explain,

but throughout the race did it, again and again.

 75

The last time he landed, his jockey yelled, 'Great!

Murray, you've done it, we're on the home straight!'

With growing excitement, and a grin on his face

Murray zoomed past the finish . . .

The crowd went bananas,

the whole place went wild;

Murray glanced over at

Tom and he smiled.

The jockey leapt up in

his saddle with zest,

shouting –

The winning horse turned to scour the crowd

and he noticed his parents, both joyful and proud.

Next to his dad he spotted the face

whose blunder had helped Murray come in first place.

The stable boy stood there and gave a sly wink;

which made Murray stop, take a moment and think . . .

Then just as the horse was about to wink back,

the stable boy turned and he walked from the track!

Still no one knows who he was to this day,

as he left without trace when he trundled away.

But one thing was certain, though the young lad was gone,

Murray ran backwards from that moment on!

They even made wing mirrors,

    smart as can be

that strapped to his head

    so that Murray could see.

He got what he dreamt of – the fortune and fame –

    and at last had the thrill of fans cheering **his name**.

Murray triumphed in races, broke records on courses

and **won the respect** of the other racehorses.

So no matter how big your ambition may seem,

keep on believing and follow your dream.

Some people out there are keen on the notion

of travelling the world or exploring the ocean!

Some yearn for stardom on stage and on screen;

others, to sing and perform for their queen.

The fact is, sometimes you'll find 'dreams do come true'

and who knows? One day it could happen to you!

But remember, your wishes, no matter how grand . . .

Might not turn out the way you had planned!